THAT'S OUR CLEO!

ABOUT THIS BOOK

Cleo liked to eat. In the evening, she appeared at the Carters' for dinner—chopped liver, maybe, or roast beef. The Carters liked to feed Cleo. They thought she was their very own cat.

But—

At breakfast time, Cleo waited at Bob and Joe's door. Bob and Joe fed her whitefish with caper sauce, or crab meat salad. They were glad to. They thought Cleo was their very own cat.

And—

Cleo always ate lunch with Grandma Green. She had a bit of meat and a vegetable and some of Grandma's delicious butter cookies. Grandma was happy to share her lunch with (she thought) her very own cat.

What would happen when the Carters and Bob and Joe and Grandma Green all found out about each other?

The story of Cleo is only one of the wonderful stories in this book about cats and the people who love them.

THAT'S OUR CLEO!

AND OTHER STORIES ABOUT CATS

cover illustration by
TOM O'SULLIVAN

illustrated by
MORRIS GOLLUB

®GOLDEN PRESS
Western Publishing Company, Inc.
Racine, Wisconsin

CONTENTS

THAT'S OUR CLEO!

Virginia B. Novinger

Cleo was a most unusual cat. She was long and sleek and as black as ink. Her slanty green eyes seemed to see everything around her, all at once. Her eyes glittered when she thought of food, and Cleo thought about food quite a good deal of the time—if not most of the time.

Her little pink tongue darted in and out of her mouth when she was hungry, and Cleo was hungry most of the time.

Cleo waited around the Carters' kitchen each evening as Mrs. Carter fixed supper. Mr. Carter called Cleo their "gourmet cat."

"Gourmets love good food. A gourmet cat— that's our Cleo!" Mr. Carter would say.

After supper, Cleo would curl up on a pillow between the kitchen stove and the refrigerator. She would sleep the night through.

The Carter twins, Chris and Tina, loved Cleo. Often they said, "Aren't we lucky to have a cat as smart as Cleo?"

However, every morning, just as surely as she had had supper at the Carters' the night before, Cleo turned up at the door of an apartment two blocks away. Two young men lived there.

The young bachelors cooked all kinds of good things. Many times they cooked fish or other kinds of seafood. Cleo liked these dishes most of all.

Some mornings she had a bit of whitefish with caper sauce. Some mornings she had creamed tuna fish. Other mornings she had crab meat salad.

Joe and Bob called their cat Juliet.

"That cat sure does like us," Bob would say.

"Sure nice to have Juliet to eat up the leftovers," Joe would reply.

Then Joe and Bob would go off to work.

Cleo would sit on their back steps and watch them as they drove out of sight. Then she would wash her face with her paws and her little pink tongue. She always rested awhile, stretching happily now and again.

Just a little before noon, Cleo would arrive at Grandma Green's house. Grandma baked cookies and breads and cakes. These were for a little restaurant down at the Neighborhood Shopping Center. HOME-BAKED DESSERTS, the sign read, BAKED BY GRANDMA GREEN.

There was one special little butter cookie that Cleo liked best. It was soft on the inside and crispy on the edges. Cleo would smell that butter cookie cooling on Grandma's table and would meow loudly, to let Grandma know she had come for lunch.

"Well, well," Grandma would say. "Here's my kitty cat, home for lunch."

Grandma Green had her main meal at noon, so Cleo had her main meal at noon, too. A bit of meat and some vegetable—Cleo liked peas best of all—then some golden butter cookies and milk.

Grandma would say, "A cat surely is comforting. It's nice to have a cat here to eat lunch with me."

Grandma called her cat Black Beauty.

After lunch, Cleo always took a long afternoon nap at Grandma Green's house. She curled up in a spot of sunlight on the parlor rug. Grandma liked to take a nap, too.

It was quiet and cozy in the little house. As the sun moved away from the spot on the rug and suppertime drew near, Cleo would stir. She would stand up and stretch and yawn. Her slanty green eyes would begin to glitter. Her little pink tongue would dart in and out of her mouth. Cleo was sure Mrs. Carter must be in her kitchen, fixing supper for the family.

Grandma didn't worry about where her cat spent the night. She had to put her bread to rise, and if she thought about it at all, she guessed Cleo probably slept under the back porch.

Then, just before supper, Cleo would show up at the Carters'. The twins would say, "Where have you been all day, Cleo?"

Mr. Carter would say, "Cats are very independent, you know, and I don't know of a more independent cat than our Cleo."

Sometimes Cleo had chopped liver for supper. Sometimes it was roast beef. Sometimes it was chicken, and, next to fish and other kinds of seafood, Cleo loved chicken best.

For quite a while, Cleo lived like a queen. Supper and the night at the Carters'. Breakfast with Joe and Bob. Lunch and a lazy afternoon at Grandma Green's.

Just one thing, however, was getting to be a

15

problem: Cleo was getting fatter and fatter. She moved much more slowly. She couldn't jump from the chair to the couch to the footstool at the Carters' as easily as she could before she became a successful gourmet cat.

Once she had enjoyed leaping from trash can to trash can behind the houses—just for the exercise, of course—but now, every once in a while, she didn't quite make it and fell down between the cans. It was very undignified, and the noise— positively frightening!

She had always enjoyed climbing up the tree over Joe and Bob's back steps. But now she was finding it hard to get even halfway up that tree. It was embarrassing to feel so fat and clumsy, especially if someone was watching.

Mrs. Carter was the first to notice Cleo's gain in weight. "Really, Cleo, on one meal a day, I don't see how you have gained so much weight. I think we'd better put you on a diet."

Joe and Bob said, "Seems funny that Juliet is

getting so fat. On one meal a day, you wouldn't think she'd get so plump. Better put her on a diet."

Grandma Green said, "I think perhaps I'd better give you cookies without butter. You are getting much too plump. And no butter on your vegetables, either. You need to go on a diet."

Cleo didn't know what a diet was, but she hoped it was something good to eat.

For the next few days, things were pretty much the same as always. Cleo's meals were a little bit smaller and not quite so rich, but they were quite enough to satisfy her.

And then something happened.

Mr. Carter had the idea first. He said, "You know, we really should take our cat to the vet. Cats should have checkups, too. Maybe the vet can tell us why Cleo is getting so fat."

Mr. Carter and the twins took Cleo to the vet's that very evening after supper.

The animal doctor was a short, dark, round

little man with a very bald head. He wore dark-rimmed glasses and peered out over the tops of them as he greeted his patients.

His Small Animal Hospital was in the Neighborhood Shopping Center, not far from the restaurant that had the sign HOME-BAKED DESSERTS, BAKED BY GRANDMA GREEN.

The vet's name was Dr. Fox, but sometimes he was called Dr. Wolf. Upon occasion he was called Dr. Lion or Dr. Tiger or even Dr. Elephant— but this he really did not like very much.

Dr. Fox looked at Cleo.

Cleo looked back with her slanty green eyes.

"What is the cat's name?" asked Dr. Fox.

"Cleo," said Mr. Carter.

Dr. Fox put Cleo's name down on a card and put the card in his cat file.

"This is a fine, healthy cat you have here, Mr. Carter. Just been letting her get too fat, that's all. Does she have her big meal at night?"

"Well, ah, yes, she does," Mr. Carter said.

"Well, then, I suggest cutting down on the size of her meal. Just a half can of cat food is enough. And a little milk. Skimmed milk. Maybe a little Kitty Kiss during the day, for a treat, but we must get the weight down."

"All right," Mr. Carter agreed. He really didn't want to tell Dr. Fox that they didn't see Cleo during the day—only at suppertime and for the night. Seemed sort of silly to say they had only a part-time cat.

So for a few days, when Cleo came for supper, she got a small dish of cat food and a little saucer of milk—skimmed.

Cleo wondered about all this—but, after all, she could still count on Joe and Bob and Grandma Green to give her two good meals a day.

She jumped from chair to couch to footstool, trying to look graceful, trying not to look fat. Once in a while, she missed the footstool and fell sprawling at Mr. Carter's feet. She pretended she'd done it on purpose, though, and walked off,

19

with her nose in the air, to find her pillow to sleep on.

Pretty soon something dreadful happened.

One morning at breakfast, just as she was swallowing the last bit of rainbow trout, broiled and boned, Joe said, "You know, Bob, I think we'd better take our cat to the vet. Wouldn't hurt to have her checked over. Maybe she needs a shot. Dogs get shots. Maybe cats should, too."

It was Bob's day off from work. He said he would take Cleo to Dr. Fox, because he was the closest vet.

Dr. Fox looked at Cleo.

Cleo looked at Dr. Fox.

"Seems I've met this cat before," Dr. Fox said.

"Oh, no, I don't think so," Bob said. "My friend and I live together, and this is our cat. We've never had her to a vet before."

Dr. Fox looked puzzled. "What is the cat's name?"

"We call her Juliet."

Dr. Fox got out a card and wrote down *Juliet*. He put the card in his cat file.

"Now. Nothing wrong with this cat. Just getting a little too fat. When do you feed her?"

"In the morning, before we go to work," Bob replied.

"Hmmmmm, well, fine. Just cut down on the size of her meal. Give her a half can of cat food and a little milk. Skimmed milk. That should be enough. Maybe a little Kitty Kiss during the day, for a treat."

Bob said all right. He did not want to tell Dr. Fox that Juliet just had breakfast with them. He didn't want to admit to a part-time cat.

Cleo listened quietly. She turned her green, slanty eyes on Dr. Fox. She glared. Dr. Fox looked back at Cleo.

"I could swear I've met this cat," he said.

"Impossible!" said Bob. "But thanks, anyway, Dr. Wolf."

"Fox!" snapped the doctor.

"Yes. Fox. Well, we will do exactly as you say."

Bob left, with Cleo under his arm.

"Sometimes I feel I'm getting very old," the doctor muttered to himself. He turned to his cat file, removed two cards, and sat staring at the names *Cleo* and *Juliet*.

For a while, Cleo's days were much the same. She got to the Carters' for supper on time. A small dish of cat food awaited her. The milk was skimmed.

She went to Joe and Bob's early in the morning for breakfast. A small dish of cat food was waiting. The milk was skimmed.

But, she would say to herself, *at least I'll get a square meal at Grandma's. Maybe she will have chicken soup today. Maybe there will be cookies. And, thank goodness, the milk is never skimmed.*

Cleo did get a little slimmer on her diet. She could jump from chair to couch to footstool at the Carters'. She had much of her old bounce.

Now she almost never landed at Mr. Carter's feet in that humiliating sprawl.

She took the leaps over trash cans gracefully once again. She was glad of this. She didn't like being undignified, and that crashing down between the cans was more than she could bear.

She even got up the tree without huffing and puffing so much.

Then one day her world came tumbling down.

Grandma Green looked at Cleo and said, "You know, Black Beauty, I read an article about cats. It says cats should be taken to the vet at least once a year for a good checkup. I think I'll take you down to Dr. Fox today. He's closest."

Cleo could hardly swallow the fifth cookie, and even the unskimmed milk didn't taste so good.

Not again! she cried to herself.

But Grandma meant it. Pretty soon she backed her old car out of the garage. She didn't even let her cat take a nap. She put Cleo beside her on the seat, and away they went to Dr. Fox, the vet who was closest.

This time, Dr. Fox couldn't even be polite.

"Now, see here, Mrs. Grandma Green! What's going on around here, fun and games? How many times do I have to see this same fat, black, slanty-green-eyed cat?"

"Now, just a moment, sir," said Grandma Green. "Whatever do you mean? This cat has never been here before now. She is my cat, and I have never had her to a vet before."

In a small, choked voice, Dr. Fox asked, "...the cat's name, please?"

"...name is Black Beauty, because that's ...e is: a lovely black beauty."

...x sat down firmly.

...k out a card and wrote *Black Beauty* ...e put the card in the cat file, then shut ...e with a loud bang.

...en he stroked his bald head.

...e put his hands over his tired eyes.

25

"Just one thing, Mrs. Grandma Green," he said. "Do you know how many fat, black, slanty-green-eyed cats there *are* in this neighborhood?"

"I have no idea," Grandma replied. "Now, see here, Dr. Wolf—"

"Fox!" roared the doctor.

"Sorry. Now, see here, Dr. Fox, are you going to look at my cat or not?"

"What is her problem? Getting fat? And, please, when does she eat her main meal?"

"Black Beauty and I eat our main meal at noon," Grandma Green stated firmly.

"That's just what I thought!" said the doctor. "Well, she is a little overweight. I think you'd better cut down on the size of her meal. Just a *spoonful* of cat food and a half cup of milk. Skimmed. No Kitty Kisses, no cookies, no treats."

Cleo glared at Dr. Fox.

Dr. Fox glared back.

"Are you sure that is enough?" Grandma wanted to know.

"Quite sure, madam," said Dr. Fox.

Grandma was a little worried, but she did not want to admit to having only a part-time cat. It didn't seem quite fair to the cat.

"Well, if you're sure," she said.

"I'm sure."

Cleo's eyes glittered until they almost threw sparks.

Dr. Fox glittered right back.

Grandma Green left, carrying Cleo. They both went home and took a good, long nap.

From then on, Cleo had real problems.

Cat food at night at the Carters'.

Cat food at Joe and Bob's in the morning.

Cat food at Grandma Green's at noon.

And skimmed milk *all* the time.

It was just too dull. Nothing tasted good. Cleo longed for a little fish, some chicken, or even a hamburger.

The Carters, Joe and Bob, and Grandma Green all noticed how slim and pretty their cat had become. She jumped and leaped gracefully. She climbed with ease. She didn't huff and puff.

And she was half-starved all the time.

After another week, Cleo decided something had to be done. She remembered a visit, a long time before, with a family who lived down on the riverbank.

This family served all sorts of spicy, fattening things—rich, red sauces on spaghetti, brown gravy on bread. Cleo had not cared much for the spicy foods, but right now, in her weakened state, even hot peppers would taste wonderful.

Cleo decided to visit the Barrettis.

She left the comfortable neighborhood. She left the Carters and Joe and Bob and Grandma Green.

The Barrettis were delighted to see her again.

"Hey," one of the Barretti children shouted, "here's That Cat again."

They had always called Cleo "That Cat."

Mamma Barretti cooked rich, red, spicy sauces

and gave them to Cleo on spaghetti.

Grandma Barretti made dark brown gravy and put some on crusts of bread for Cleo.

Down here at the riverbank, the milk was *never* skimmed. In fact, it came right from the Barrettis' own cow, and, as often as not, Cleo had it while it was still warm!

Ohhh, heaven! thought Cleo.

Cleo stayed in heaven for four days. She ate and she slept, and then she ate some more. Her sides got plump and round again. Her green eyes glittered, and her little pink tongue darted in and out of her mouth.

The fifth day, along about suppertime, Cleo decided to take a walk. She was lonely and figured it wouldn't hurt to walk past the Carters'.

She walked up the riverbank, out through the little grove of trees, and onto the main street back into town.

She had not gone too far when it happened!

At the corner of High and Low streets, in the

Neighborhood Shopping Center, Cleo stopped short, her eyes darting this way and that.

Coming toward her from one direction was Mr. Carter, carrying a big bag of groceries.

Coming from the other direction was Joe. He carried a pail of water, and out of the water stuck a tasty-looking lobster claw.

Walking along the other side of the street, toward the restaurant, was Grandma Green. She carried a big box, and Cleo knew it must be filled with butter cookies.

Mr. Carter saw her first. "Cleo!" he shouted.

And then, "Juliet!" yelled Joe.

"Black Beauty!" screeched Grandma Green.

Cleo didn't know what to do.

Run? Which way?

Hide? Where?

Just then the door of the Small Animal Hospital opened, and there stood Dr. Fox.

Cleo took one dive and skidded between the short, fat legs of the vet, almost upsetting him.

She ran behind the counter, streaked into the doctor's office, and hid under the far corner of his desk, scrunching down to make herself as small as possible.

Dr. Fox ran for his cat file.

"I'm going to get to the bottom of this!" he roared.

Mr. Carter came in shouting, "Cleo!"

Joe came in yelling, "Juliet!"

Grandma Green came in screeching, "Black Beauty!"

Dr. Fox sat down very slowly. The three cards from his cat file dropped from his hand.

Dr. Fox put his head in his hands. "Yes, I do feel very old," he said.

Cleo stayed under Dr. Fox's desk.

She didn't know quite what to do. She didn't feel at all well. She wished she weren't so full of rich, red, spicy spaghetti sauce.

They were all talking at once now. Mr. Carter was saying something about Cleo and the evening

32

meal. "And she sleeps at our house, too," he added.

Joe was telling about how he and Bob shared this apartment and had always welcomed Juliet to their breakfast table. "Well, not *really* the table . . ." he said.

Grandma Green was saying, "Yes, Black Beauty and I always have our main meal at noon, but she hasn't been home for several days. It's been lonely without her, too."

Dr. Fox listened for a while. Then he rose to his full height of five feet five inches and said in a loud voice, "Quiet . . . quiet, everybody!"

They all stopped talking. They all looked at Dr. Fox.

"Folks," he said, "you may not believe this, but you have all been the innocent victims of a very, very cunning cat."

"What?"

"What?"

"What?"

"Yes, folks. I think I've finally got this thing figured out."

Cleo had it figured out, too. She figured she had better get out of that office and back to the Barrettis'. The food was a little spicy, but she had found that a drink of water sort of put out the fire, so to speak. Most important, she didn't have to feel like a criminal for eating well at the Barrettis'!

But Cleo did not know Dr. Fox.

As she edged around his chair, getting ready to spring for the door, the doctor leaned over and scooped Cleo up in his hands.

Dr. Fox looked at Cleo.

Cleo-Juliet-Black Beauty looked at him.

Their eyes glittered.

"That's our Cleo!" shouted Mr. Carter.

"That's Juliet!" yelled Joe.

"That's Black Beauty!" screeched Grandma Green.

"That's *right!*" said Dr. Fox.

Well, I've had it, thought Cleo-Juliet-Black Beauty.

"Tell you what we'd better do," Dr. Fox said at last.

"Yes?"

"Yes?"

"Yes?"

"You all liked the idea of having a part-time cat, didn't you?"

"Oh, yes," they all said at once.

Mr. Carter said, "The twins are in school all day, and we like having Cleo for supper. We enjoy having her spend the night."

Joe said, "Bob and I work all day, so breakfast with Juliet is fine with us."

Grandma Green said, "Black Beauty and I just enjoy our meal at noon and our nap afterward."

Dr. Fox said, "I don't see anything the matter with keeping things that way, do you?"

They all agreed that it was a good idea.

35

"There's just one thing," Dr. Fox said. "We must plan some sort of diet that will be right for Cleo . . . er, Juliet . . . er, Black Beauty."

"Yes, she's quite a gourmet," Mr. Carter said with a smile.

"So!" said Dr. Fox. "Mr. Carter, for supper, cat food and skimmed milk."

"All right," said Mr. Carter.

"Joe," Dr. Fox said, "for breakfast, a little fish or some tasty leftover and some skimmed milk."

"Okay, Dr. Wolf," said Joe.

"Fox!" screamed the doctor.

"Oh, yes. Sorry."

"And Grandma Green," Dr. Fox said, "no cookies. Just a bit of cottage cheese, perhaps, or a little meat at noon. Some vegetable that she likes, maybe. But *no cat food* at noon. You can give her a Kitty Kiss before she leaves for the Carters', though, I should think."

"All right," said Grandma Green.

Dr. Fox had been holding Cleo. They looked

each other right in the eyes. Then he put Cleo on the floor at his feet. She rubbed her plump, black sides against his leg.

"I think even Cleo . . . er, Juliet . . . er, Black Beauty feels that our plan is all right."

Dr. Fox took up the three cards. He clipped them all together with a paper clip. He put them in his cat file.

"Let's see, now," he said. "It's almost suppertime. You can take her home with you, eh, Mr. Carter?"

"Oh, yes," Mr. Carter said. "The twins will be so glad to have her back. We've missed her."

Joe said, "Well, see you in the morning, Juliet. We're having lobster tonight!"

Grandma Green said, "Come for lunch, Black Beauty."

They all left the Small Animal Hospital. Mr. Carter carried his sack of groceries in one arm and Cleo in the other.

Joe carried his bucket of lobster.

37

Grandma Green carried the cookies over to the restaurant.

And Cleo-Juliet-Black Beauty decided that being on a diet didn't sound so bad, after all.

Besides, when it got a little dull, she could always go down to the riverbank. The Barrettis would give her a dish of rich, red, spicy spaghetti sauce.

With a smug little grin, Cleo snuggled against Mr. Carter and thought about supper.

THE CAREFUL CAT

Ellen M. Dolan

Ann sang happily to herself. They were moving to Spring Falls today. As soon as the car stopped in front of her new home there, she flung open the door and jumped out. She ran up the steps to the wide front porch. Something special awaited her in this new house.

Father had come earlier with the moving men. He stood on the porch, looking pleased as he waited for Ann and Mother.

Ann called, "Oh, Father, where is it? Where is it?"

Father smiled and stepped aside. "First one

on the left, down the hallway," he said.

Ann ran past him and down the hall. At the first door on the left, she stopped.

"Oh," she said softly.

The room was big and bright. Sun shone on the pale yellow walls. The windows were wide and looked out on the woods behind the house.

Ann hugged herself and danced around.

"It's a beautiful room," she cried. "And it's all mine!"

For the first time in her eight years, Ann was to have a room all her own. She had always shared a room with her twelve-year-old sister, Susan. Now Susan was spending the summer with Aunt Barbara, in the city.

Ann pushed open the windows and looked out. How she loved trees, woods, animals—anything that belonged outdoors.

"I must go out and see those woods—right now!" she said.

"Not yet," said Father from the hall. "Mother

needs help, and I must go to work."

"All right," said Ann with a sigh. Slowly she closed the windows and looked around again at her new room. Then she went to find Mother.

Mother was unpacking dishes in the kitchen.

"Shall I unpack, too?" asked Ann.

"Oh, goodness, no. Not you," said Mother. "You may bring in the small bundles from the car. And—please be careful."

"Be careful, be careful," said Ann on the way to the car. "Susan tells me to be careful, but she's not here now. Father tells me to be careful, but he's gone to work. Now Mother tells me to be careful. Bother!"

She opened the car door and reached in for a small suitcase. One of the locks was open. Susan would have closed it before she picked up the case, but Ann was thinking about the woods.

She started up the steps. *Whang!* The lid of the suitcase popped open, and all the clothes fell out.

41

"Oh, dear," said Mother from the doorway. "I told you to be careful, Ann."

"Bother," sighed Ann as she picked up the things.

For the rest of the afternoon, Ann tried to be very careful. She stored cans on shelves. She folded towels.

"You're a big help, Ann," said Mother in a pleased voice.

Ann would much rather be helping Father. His work was fun. He was an archaeologist and spent his days digging for spears or dishes left by ancient people.

Ann liked to look for things, too. Someday she hoped to be an archaeologist, like Father. But how could she learn, if he never let her help?

At Spring Falls, Father was going to look for traces of Indians who had lived long ago. How Ann wished she could find something important for Father. Then he would let her help.

After dinner, Ann went right to her new room. "Being careful is such a bother that I'm tired," she said. "How nice to have my own room. Nobody will keep me awake tonight." Ann yawned and got into bed.

She thought she would fall asleep right away in her pretty new room. She was surprised to find how quiet the room was. Too quiet.

Ann had never before known that it was so dark at night. She had never before heard so many creaks in a house. She had never before slept alone in a room.

Ann sat up in bed and looked around the room. Moonlight shone through the windows and made shadows everywhere. She wished that Susan were here or that Mother would come in. She covered her head with the blankets and lay down.

"I wish I had someone to sleep with me," Ann said into the blankets, "or something soft and warm to snuggle."

43

Suddenly she sat up again. Something soft and warm. That was it! A kitten! The room wouldn't seem so lonely if there were a cuddly, purring kitten in bed with her at night. They could play in the woods during the day, too.

"I'm glad I thought of a kitten. I'll ask Mother in the morning." Now the room didn't seem so quiet, and soon she was asleep.

At breakfast next morning, Ann said, "Mother, my new room is very pretty."

"I'm glad you like it, Ann," said Mother.

"But it's so quiet at night. Do you think I could have something to keep me company?"

Mother looked surprised. "I thought you wanted to be alone."

"I didn't know it would be so quiet. If I had a kitten. . . ."

"A kitten," said Mother thoughtfully. "Yes, that might be the thing." She looked at Father.

Father smiled and nodded.

"Yes, Ann," said Mother. "I'm going into

44

town to shop this morning. Come with me and look for a kitten."

"Oh, thank you," said Ann, pushing back her chair.

"Be careful!" said Father as the chair tipped.

"Oh, dear me," Mother sighed as the chair crashed to the floor.

"Bother," said Ann as she picked it up.

When Father left for work, Ann and Mother got into the car. All the way to town, Ann thought about the kitten. She knew just the kind she wanted. Her cousin Julie had a cat that didn't like to be held. That was not the kind of cat for Ann.

When they got to town, Mother said, "I'll shop while you look for your kitten. Be careful."

Carefully Ann crossed Main Street. Then she saw a pet shop and forgot all about being careful. She ran all the way to the door.

"Hello," Ann said breathlessly to the man in the shop. "I'm looking for a kitten that wants to

45

be held. Do you have one?"

"I just got three brand-new kittens," said the man. He brought a big box to Ann.

Ann looked into the box at the kittens.

"How soft they look," she said.

She reached out toward the kittens, to pick one up. All three scurried to the farthest corner.

"They're afraid." Ann was disappointed.

"Give them time," said the man. "You're a stranger to them."

Ann tried to be patient. She talked softly to the kittens. She held out her hand. But the kittens stayed in the corner.

"Bother," sighed Ann at last. "These kittens don't want to be held. Do you have any others?"

"Just one," said the man. "A full-grown Siamese cat."

Ann really wanted a kitten, but maybe a grown cat was ready to be held. "May I see it?" she asked.

The man brought a brown and cream-colored

cat with deep blue eyes. He put him on the counter.

"What a beautiful cat," said Ann. "Oh, I hope he likes me."

She reached out. The cat stepped back, but Ann didn't stop. She picked him up and put him on her shoulder. The cat looked at her. He mewed loudly and jumped back to the counter, shaking himself crossly, as if to straighten his fur.

"Please come to me," said Ann.

The cat didn't even look at her.

"This cat doesn't want to be held, either. What shall I do?" Ann asked.

"I have no more cats here," said the man. "You might find one at a farm."

Ann thanked him and left the shop. She met Mother and told her she had no kitten . . . that she couldn't find one that wanted to be held.

"I'm sorry," said Mother. "We'll see what Father can do."

"Oh, I hope he can find one," said Ann. She was quiet on the ride home. She was quiet as she helped put the groceries away.

Father came home for lunch. He stood in the doorway and looked at Ann. "What a gloomy face," he said. "We must fix that. I have a present."

Ann dropped a bag of sugar. "Oh, Father, you have a cat for me!"

"A cat?" said Father in surprise. "I have no cat. I have a package. It's for someone who wants to be an archaeologist."

"That's me, that's me!" shouted Ann, jumping up and down.

"Wait," said Father. "An archaeologist must learn to be very, very careful. The things he finds can break very easily. Do you still want to be one?"

"Oh, yes," said Ann. "I can learn to be more careful. I know I can."

Father smiled and handed her a long box.

Ann carefully opened the lid.

"A digging kit!" she cried.

She picked up a small shovel. It was just her size. Inside the kit were brushes for pushing aside dirt, a flashlight for searching dark places, and plaster of Paris for making casts of footprints.

"I know I'll find something important now," said Ann.

"We'll see," said Father. "Now, what's this about a cat?"

Ann was so busy with her new tools that she had almost forgotten about the cat. Quickly she told Father about her visit to the pet shop and her disappointment.

Father promised to ask at a farm the next day. Ann, he said, would just have to learn to be patient.

After lunch Ann asked, "May I go out and dig?"

"Yes," said Mother, "but be—"

"I know," said **Ann**, laughing. "I'll be careful."

She knew where she wanted to dig. In those woods. From her window, she had seen a spot halfway up the hill.

Ann ran to the edge of the woods. An old path led upward through the trees. She followed it until she came to a clearing. On one side, she could look down and see her house. From the other side, she could see Father and the men digging by the river.

"This is a good place to dig," said Ann in a voice like Father used. "Where shall I start?"

Father always drew a checkerboard on the ground before he started to dig. Then he worked it one square at a time.

"I must draw carefully," said Ann.

So, very carefully, she began to draw on the ground with her shovel. Soon she got tired.

"Being careful is hot work," she said.

But at last Ann was finished. She began to dig in the first square. In a moment, with a ping, her shovel hit something. Ann got a brush and gently moved the dust away from the object. Was this a spearhead?

"Oh, it's only a rock," said Ann. She put it aside and began to dig again.

Suddenly she heard a noise in the woods.

"Who's there?" she called.

Nobody answered. There was a crackle of leaves. Ann looked between the trees, but nobody was there. She jumped up and started down the hill.

Then she stopped. Two yellow eyes were staring at her from the woods. Slowly an animal crept out onto the path in front of her.

"A cat," she said with relief. "Nothing but a cat!" Then, softly, "What are you doing in the woods?"

This was the strangest cat Ann had ever seen. He was nothing like the cats at the pet shop. His head was very big. He had wide, wide shoulders and one droopy ear. His fur was orange and white striped, matted and tangled with burrs. He looked like a fighter.

"You won't want to be held," said Ann.

This cat didn't look soft or cuddly, but he did look lonely and frightened and very thin. Ann longed to pick him up.

But she had learned about cats that morning. Now she was very careful. She didn't move toward him. She didn't even hold out a hand. She picked up her shovel and went back to work, but she kept watching the cat.

He walked around and around Ann. Then he came closer. He knew how to be careful, too. At last he sat down nearby and watched her. Ann lifted her hand to stroke his poor fur.

Then she drew back. "I'll wait until you know me better," she said.

Ann went on digging and brushing away dust. The cat watched her, without moving. Then suddenly he put his paw in the dust and slowly began to brush it aside.

53

"Do you like to dig, too?" Ann asked, surprised but pleased.

The cat moved more dust aside. Ann reached over and touched his back. She could feel him stiffen, and he looked around at her. Then he lay down on the ground. He stretched out. He seemed to like it. Ann stroked him until she heard Mother call.

"Time for dinner," said Ann. "You must be hungry, too."

Pretending not to notice the cat, Ann picked up her kit and started for home. The cat wailed softly, watching Ann anxiously as she moved off.

Ann turned and held out her hand. Slowly the cat began to follow her.

"Good," said Ann. "Maybe I can get you to leave the woods."

The cat followed her down the hill and across the backyard. He stood and looked at the house for a long time. Then he sat down on the porch steps and looked up at her.

54

"You are careful," said Ann. She held the door open. "Come in. We won't hurt you."

But the cat didn't move. Even when Ann went in, he just sat there. Then he wailed again, piteously.

"I have to go in," said Ann from the doorway. "I live here."

Still the cat wouldn't follow her, so Ann went to get Mother. "Mother, I found a strange cat. He won't come in. May I have some milk for him?"

"Why, of course, dear," said Mother. "What kind of cat is it?"

"A careful cat," said Ann. "He lives in the woods, and he likes to dig."

"I must see this cat," said Mother.

Ann poured milk in a saucer, filling it as full as she could without its running over.

"Oh, dear," said Mother when she saw the cat, but she caught herself and managed an imitation bright smile at him.

Ann put the saucer in front of the cat. He looked at it, sniffed, but didn't drink. Then, slowly, he put one paw in the saucer. He licked the paw. He dipped it back in the milk and licked again. At last he put his head down and began to lap the milk thirstily, making little smacking noises.

"He *is* careful," said Mother. "What a funny way to drink milk."

"Maybe he's never had milk in a saucer before," said Ann.

She picked up the empty saucer and went for more milk. Mother went inside, too. When Ann came back, the porch was empty.

The cat was gone.

"Oh, where did he go?" cried Ann. "I thought he was beginning to like me."

Ann hadn't even held the cat yet, but she knew he was the one she wanted. He was all alone. She must find him. She started heading for the woods.

"Ann, come back," called Mother. "It's getting dark, and it looks like rain."

"But I *have* to find the cat," said Ann. "Please let me look for him."

"Just for a few minutes," said Mother.

Ann ran to the woods. She went back to her digging place. She called and called. She looked and looked. But she couldn't find the cat. Big drops of rain were falling before she gave up.

Father was coming home, too. Ann met him in the yard.

"Hurry," he said. "You'll get wet."

"Oh, Father," said Ann. "I found a cat. Then he ran away, back to the woods. He's all alone out there in the rain!"

"A woods cat," said Father thoughtfully. "Do you really think he's the kind you want? Or shall I ask at a farm tomorrow?"

"This is the one I want. He needs to be held," said Ann. "Do you think he'll come back?"

"It might be hard for a woods cat to live in

a house, but I think he'll come back if he likes you," said Father. "Now, don't worry."

But Ann did worry. She couldn't help it. She was already thinking of the woods cat as her own.

It was raining hard by the time Ann went to bed. She could think only of the cat, all alone in the wet woods. The lightning made her room seem even lonelier than it had the night before. Ann tried to cover her ears to shut out a loud wailing sound.

Suddenly she sat up. She had heard that wail before! She ran to the window. Sitting on the windowsill, out in the wind and rain, was the cat. She opened the window, and he jumped into the room, still making unhappy little sounds.

His fur was flattened, and he was shivering. He looked worse than ever.

Quickly Ann ran to get a towel. She dried the cat carefully. Then she brushed the burrs and tangles out of his fur. He seemed to like being brushed. He even rolled over so she could do his stomach.

When she had finished, Ann sat back to look at the cat. What a surprise! His fur was shiny and silken. His tail was soft and feathery. His stripes were bright. Even his ear didn't seem to droop so much.

"You're beautiful," said Ann. She had to hug him, and the cat didn't mind a bit. "A handsome cat like you needs a name," she said. "I'm going to call you Sergeant. You have such pretty stripes, and you're used to fighting your way alone."

Ann sat down on the bed. She waited to see what Sergeant would do now. He came over and rubbed against her leg. He walked around the room. He seemed restless. Then he jumped up on the windowsill, lay down, and stared out at the rain.

Ann was disappointed. She wanted to put him in bed with her, but he might not like that.

"You're just not used to a house yet," she said. "But at least you're warm and dry."

Ann soon fell asleep.

When she awoke the next morning, the sun was shining brightly again. Sergeant was washing his face. He looked up when Ann moved.

"Good morning," Ann said softly. "Do you want to dig again today? Maybe we'll find something."

"Meow," said Sergeant. He looked out the window. Ann opened it. The cat jumped through and ran off toward the woods.

"Wait!" called Ann. She climbed through the window and hurried after him. But she was too late. Sergeant had disappeared again.

"Do you think he'll come back?" Ann asked at breakfast.

"I hope so, Ann," said Mother.

"If he likes you," said Father again.

"I don't think he knows yet. He's careful about making friends, too," said Ann.

61

As soon as she could, Ann got her digging kit and hurried to her spot in the woods. Sergeant wasn't waiting at the clearing. Perhaps he would come back to her while she was working. She began to dig.

Carefully she worked the last square of the checkerboard. She had found only rocks and tin cans. Suddenly she heard a noise behind her. She turned. Nothing was there. She heard it again— a long, high wail.

"That's Sergeant! He's in trouble!" said Ann.

But where was he? Ann looked under rocks and behind trees. She listened again. Sergeant's wails seemed to come from a clump of bushes beside the path.

Ann poked in the bushes. She looked behind them. And then she stopped. There in the side of the hill was a small crack. It was just big enough for an animal like Sergeant to slip through. He sounded closer now.

Ann put her eyes to the crack. It was very

dark inside. "Come out, Sergeant, come out," she called.

But Sergeant just wailed again. He sounded very frightened.

"I must help him," said Ann, "quickly."

She pushed her arm into the crack, but she couldn't feel anything. "I must think of something," she said. "Sergeant may be in danger!"

Suddenly she thought of her digging kit. She ran to it and tumbled everything onto the ground. "My flashlight! And my shovel! Good," said Ann.

She ran back to the crack and turned her light into it. Then she gasped and stepped back.

"A cave! A huge, black cave," said Ann. "No wonder Sergeant could disappear so fast."

She still couldn't see him, but she could hear him.

"I'm coming, Sergeant," called Ann. She got her shovel and began to push at the sides of the crack. Dirt and rocks fell away, and soon the crack was bigger. Ann kept working. Her arms were covered with mud and getting tired. Her hair had fallen over her eyes. But she must see what was happening to Sergeant.

At last the crack was big enough for Ann to see into the opening, without going inside. That, she knew, was something she must not do. "Explorers," Father often told her, "never go into caves alone. Not ever!"

Ann lay down on her stomach. She flashed her light along the floor of the big cave. Sergeant wasn't there. Nothing was on the floor but an old broken dish.

Suddenly Ann moved the light back to the dish. It was red and blue with black markings on it.

"An old Indian dish!" said Ann excitedly. "Wait until I show this to Father."

Sergeant wailed again. He sounded more frightened than ever. Now Ann could tell where he was. She turned the light to the left.

64

High on a narrow ledge stood Sergeant. His back was arched in fear. His eyes were shining, and his fur was stiff.

Glaring up at him was a red fox.

"A fox!" breathed Ann.

This was one time Sergeant couldn't fight alone, and Ann was frightened herself. How could she chase that fox away?

Then Ann remembered that Father was working close by. "I'll be right back, Sergeant," she called. "Stay there!"

Then she started down the hill toward Father. Faster and faster she ran. Bushes tore her shirt. Dust flew in her face. But all she could think of was Sergeant. He would be safe only as long as he stayed on the ledge. At last she reached the bottom of the hill. Father was working nearby.

He looked at her torn clothing and muddy face, then threw down his tools. "What's the matter, Ann? What happened to you?"

"Sergeant is in a cave up on the hill. A fox

65

is trying to get him," gasped Ann, out of breath.

"A cave? Up on the hill?" said Father in surprise. He turned to the men. "Bring your shovels and come with us."

Ann led the men up the hill. She wished they would hurry. Was Sergeant still on that ledge? It had looked so small. Had the fox reached him yet? She ran faster.

Just as they all burst into the clearing, the fox put his head out of the crack.

"There he is," said Ann. "He heard us coming."

The fox looked at the men and the shovels. For a minute he held back, frightened. Then he leaped out of the cave and dashed into the woods.

"Oh, thank goodness," said Ann. "Now we've got to get to Sergeant. Can you get into the cave?"

Father and the men looked at the crack. Then they got busy. Soon dirt and rock were flying. The crack became a big doorway into the cave.

Father shone his light into the opening.

"Wait, Father," said Ann as he started to go in. "I think there's an Indian dish on the floor. Don't step on it."

Father smiled. "Ann, you're learning to be careful. However, I'm always careful in a cave. Where is the dish?"

Ann flashed her light on the ground. Father saw the piece of pottery and knelt down. "It is an old Indian dish!" he exclaimed. "Good girl, Ann!"

The men crowded behind Ann so they could see, too.

"Please, Father," said Ann, "is Sergeant all right?"

Sergeant cried out very weakly. At least he was still alive.

"Come down, Sergeant," Ann called soothingly. "The fox is gone."

"He can't get down," said Father. "He's climbed too high. I'll have to go get him. Hold your light on the wall while I climb."

"Be careful," said Ann. Father laughed.

Ann held her light steadily on the cave wall. To her surprise, she saw small holes in it.

Father used the holes as he climbed. He reached for Sergeant. The cat hissed and backed up closer to the wall, but finally Father got him and climbed down. He brought Sergeant to Ann.

She put him on her shoulder and stroked him. "You'll never be alone again," she whispered softly. "I'll take care of you now." At last Sergeant's trembling stopped.

Now that Sergeant was safe, Ann remembered the holes. She turned her light back on the wall.

"Look, Father," she said. "Those holes in the wall over there look just like steps!"

Father looked, too. Then he got very excited. He called to the men. Ann stood in the sunshine and looked into the cave in amazement. Men were hurrying from wall to wall. They were pointing at the floor. Lights shone everywhere.

Voices called in excited tones. Something was happening.

Then Father came out to Ann. His eyes were shining. "Ann, I think you've made an important discovery. Those steps were to an ancient house. It looks as if there's an entire Indian village in this cave. Come in and see."

Ann followed Father into the cave. He shone his light high across the walls. Row upon row of ancient houses stood next to each other.

Ann gasped with wonder. Indians had played here once, had cooked and eaten their food, had put their children to bed—all so long ago!

Ann's heart beat faster. So this was how an archaeologist felt when he found something important. She stood staring at the city until Sergeant mewed sorrowfully. She held him tighter. "You must be hungry," Ann said softly, stroking his silky fur. "Father," she called, "I'm going to take Sergeant home."

"I'll be along soon," said Father. "We want

to look some more today. We'll start working in the cave tomorrow. Would you like to help?"

"Oh, Father, could I? And Sergeant, too? He's very careful."

Father laughed. "Yes, he can help. It's his cave."

Ann hurried down the hill. She held Sergeant close to her all the way. But he began to squirm when they reached her yard. She put him down and walked to the back door.

Sergeant followed closely. At the door he stopped. Ann went in, leaving the door open.

Sergeant looked after her. He put his head through the doorway and looked around the kitchen very carefully. He didn't see any fox. At last he made up his mind. With his head held high, Sergeant marched through the door and wound around Ann's ankles. He made soft, friendly noises.

"Oh, you do love me," said Ann happily. She picked him up and danced around the room.

That night when it was time for bed, Sergeant followed Ann to her room. At last he seemed at home there. When Ann got into bed, he jumped right in with her. He bounced back and forth across her. He walked on her stomach. He tickled her toes. Then he lay down very close to her, his purr a low, contented rumble.

Ann sighed. "Oh, you feel so soft. What fun we're going to have!" she said. "I'm glad you were careful about me. Now I know you'll always love me."

Mother and Father came in to say good night.

"You're going to be a fine archaeologist," said Father.

"You took time to be careful at the cave, even when Sergeant was in danger," said Mother. "We're very proud of you."

Ann looked at their happy faces, then around her pretty room, then at her fighter cat. "From now on, I'm going to be just as careful as Sergeant. I don't think it will be too hard."

Sergeant reached up to touch Ann's cheek with his paw. He purred way down in the back of his throat. He seemed to be saying, "It will be easy."

THOSE CATS!

Virginia Cunningham

Miss Simpson looked hopefully out the front window. She moved the red geraniums so that she could look all the way down the street.

What was that?

Yes, it was! It was Mr. Tooks, the postman. Miss Simpson hurried out the front door and down to the gate.

"Good morning, Mr. Tooks," she called. "Any mail for me today?"

Mr. Tooks shifted the heavy mailbag and leaned against the gatepost. "Well, now, let's

74

see," he said. He wet his thumb against his tongue and began sorting through the letters. "Two for Miss James . . . one for Doc Brown . . . and one for Mrs. Hilton, from her son up in Coal City . . . a couple of bills for Hank Peters . . . and . . . and that's all for this street. Nothing for you, Miss Simpson. Sorry."

"Oh," said Miss Simpson, trying not to sound disappointed. "Oh, well, that's all right."

"You waiting for something special?" asked Mr. Tooks. "Nothing wrong with your brother's family, I hope."

"No-o," said Miss Simpson. "Well, that is . . . I asked my niece to come and live with me, but she decided to take a job in the city instead. I told her to write to me if she changed her mind. It looks as if she hasn't, though. It's all right, of course, but . . . well . . . I'm lonely! I'm tired of living all by myself in this great big house."

"Hmm," said Mr. Tooks. He pushed his hat to the back of his head and pulled his left ear, the way he always did when he was trying to think.

"That's too bad," he said after he had thought a bit. "But 'tain't hopeless. Tell you what you need—a nice cat!"

"A cat!" said Miss Simpson. "Why, I've never had a cat in my life."

"All the more reason to get one now," said Mr. Tooks. "There's nothing like a cat for company. You can talk to it when you want to, and when you don't want to, you don't have to. It's neat and clean, and it'll catch mice. Don't know what more you could ask."

"But I—" began Miss Simpson.

"Take my word for it," Mr. Tooks said. "I know all about living alone, and I know cats. Why, my cat, Susie, is the best friend I've ever had. You should see her run to me when I come home from work. And talk about purring!"

"I'm sure she's very nice," said Miss Simpson politely, "but—"

"Yes, she is nice," Mr. Tooks said quickly,

"and so are her kittens. She has two kittens right now—an orange-colored one and a black and white one. Which one do you think would be prettier?"

"Why," said Miss Simpson, still trying to be polite, "they're probably both pretty."

"Good!" said Mr. Tooks. "That's what I hoped you'd say. Only thing better'n one cat is two cats. I'm right pleased, Miss Simpson. And I know you will be, too. Well, good-bye for now. See you after lunch."

He was off down the street before Miss Simpson could guess what he meant.

What is he so pleased about? she thought. *What does he mean?*

But she couldn't stand out by the gate wondering about Mr. Tooks, no matter how puzzled she was. She earned her living by taking in sewing, and she had to get busy.

Miss Simpson worked hard all morning. She worked so hard that she forgot all about Mr.

77

Tooks. At noon she stopped for lunch.

She had just finished eating when the doorbell rang. Three long rings and a quick one.

"Why," said Miss Simpson, "that's Mr. Tooks's ring. Perhaps he found a letter for me, after all." She hurried to the door.

"Hello," said Mr. Tooks. "Here they are."

"Who?" asked Miss Simpson. But she had a queer feeling that she knew the answer.

Mr. Tooks turned sideways so that she could see the big brown leather mailbag on his back.

Over the edge peeked a little furry orange face. Right beside it was a black and white face.

"Oh," said Miss Simpson. "Oh, my!"

"Here you are," said Mr. Tooks. He swung the bag off his shoulder, took out the kittens, and handed them to Miss Simpson.

Without knowing just how it happened, Miss Simpson found herself with a wiggly, fuzzy kitten in each hand.

She took a deep breath. "But I don't want two

cats!" she said firmly, and she tightened her lips so hard that her chin wiggled.

The orange kitten cocked its head on one side. Then it reached up a soft, furry paw and patted the wiggling chin.

The black and white kitten began to nibble on Miss Simpson's dress buttons.

"Say, now," said Mr. Tooks, beaming fondly. "Isn't that cute! They want you, all right. Why don't you just keep them awhile? If you don't like them after a week or so, I'll take them back."

"Well," said Miss Simpson slowly. "Well . . . I guess that's fair enough. But one cat is plenty. I'll try just one cat."

"Two are easier to take care of," said Mr. Tooks. "They'll keep each other company. And they'll keep each other clean, too."

"Just one," said Miss Simpson firmly.

Mr. Tooks shrugged his shoulders. Then a sly twinkle came into his eyes. "Which one?" he asked.

Those Cats!

Miss Simpson thought about the orange kitten's soft paw lightly patting her chin. "The or—" she began.

Just then the black and white kitten started to purr. It was the friendliest sound that Miss Simpson had ever heard.

"The black—" she started to say, but Mr. Tooks was talking again, at high speed.

"Shame to part them," he was saying. "They sure will miss each other. Never been apart a day in their lives. Too bad you can't take them both. My, they'll be lonely."

Miss Simpson began to feel as cruel as a wicked witch in a fairy tale.

"Of course," Mr. Tooks went on, "if you can't afford to feed two cats, I wouldn't want you to take them and let them starve."

"Starve!" said Miss Simpson. "Oh, I'd never do that. I can feed them both, but—"

"That's good!" said Mr. Tooks heartily. "That's fine. I'm glad you decided to take them both. I know you'll be very happy—all three of you. Good-bye, now."

The next minute he was through the gate and halfway down the street.

"Mr. Tooks, Mr. Tooks," called Miss Simpson. He didn't seem to hear her.

"Oh, my," said Miss Simpson. She looked down at the kittens. They were both purring as steadily as little teakettles.

"Well, I declare," she said. "Two cats. What will I do with them?"

Miss Simpson took the kittens into the kitchen and put them on the floor. They stared around at the strange room with curious, frightened eyes, but they were far more curious than they were frightened. In a minute they started to look around their new home. They sniffed at the stove legs, at the table, and at all the chair legs. They crawled under the refrigerator and peeked out at Miss Simpson like tigers in a den.

What shall I name them? thought Miss Simpson as she fixed a bed for them beside the stove. She began to say all the cat names she had ever heard of—Smoky, Snowball, Inky. No, those names didn't fit. The black and white kitten had too much white fur to be called Inky and too much black fur to be called Snowball. She was white all down the front and up on her shoulders. She looked as if she were wearing an apron, a white pinafore apron.

"Pinafore!" said Miss Simpson. "That's what I'll call you—Pinafore. Pinnie for short."

Then she looked for the orange kitten. Of course, an orange kitten couldn't be named Snowball or Inky. And she wasn't smoky-colored, either. She was—why, she was just the color of orange marmalade!

"Marmalade," Miss Simpson said aloud. "That's a good name for an orange kitten. Here, Pinnie. Here, Marmalade," she called.

At the friendly sound of her voice, the kittens came running. They sniffed at her fingers. Miss

Simpson stroked their soft fur and tickled them under their chins. The kittens liked that. They purred and rubbed their heads against Miss Simpson's hand.

Just then a fly came buzzing along. Pinafore dashed after it, but Marmalade started to explore the wastebasket. She put her paws up on the edge and looked in. Pinafore came over, too. *Bang!* Over toppled the wastebasket. *Clatter, bang, crash!*

Pinafore and Marmalade scooted behind the stove. They looked the other way, as if they had never seen the wastebasket. Then they began to wash their paws. When Marmalade had finished washing her own paws, she reached over and began to lick Pinafore's ears. The black and white kitten purred happily. She shut her eyes and curled her tail around her feet. Marmalade's eyes shut, too. In a few moments they were both sound asleep.

Miss Simpson went back to her sewing. Whirr-r-r went the motor of her electric sewing machine. *I wonder if the cats will think I'm purring, too,* thought Miss Simpson.

The blue curtains Miss Simpson was making took a long time. At last one pair was done. She got up and went over to her worktable to get the second pair. When she turned back, the blue curtain she had just finished was in a heap on the floor.

All of a sudden it puffed up like a balloon. It went whirling around in a circle, as if it were alive.

Just then the orange kitten came into the room. She stared at the whirling curtain. She crouched low—then, jump! She landed on it with all four feet at once. *R-r-r-rip!* The blue curtain tore in two. Out of the rip popped Pinafore. She went chasing after Marmalade as fast as she could go, and Miss Simpson went chasing after both of them.

Those cats! she thought. *Oh, those naughty*

cats! I'll give them back to Mr. Tooks the first thing tomorrow.

A big red spool rolled right under Miss Simpson's foot. *Wham!* Down she went.

When she looked around for the kittens, they were huddled under a chair. They looked so scared that Miss Simpson couldn't help feeling sorry for them.

"Here, kitty, kitty," she called. "You couldn't help it. Don't be frightened. Just be glad I didn't fall on you."

But the kittens didn't move. They shrank back farther under the chair.

Miss Simpson couldn't bear to have anything afraid of her—not even naughty cats that she was going to send home tomorrow.

"I know what kitties like," she said. "Some warm milk. Come, kitties."

She went out into the kitchen and fixed the warm milk. She poured some into a white dish. That was for Pinafore. Then she poured some into a yellow dish. That was for Marmalade.

"Here, kitty, kitty," she called again.

The kittens could smell the warm milk. They came out from under the chair and began to drink. But they both drank out of the yellow dish. Lap-lap-lap went their little pink tongues. Lap-lap-lap. When the yellow dish was empty, they both drank out of the white dish next to it. Their tails stood straight up in the air, side by side.

When the milk was all gone, Miss Simpson put the kittens out in the backyard to play for a while.

Thank goodness there's a high fence, she thought. *They can't get into mischief, and I won't have to worry about their getting away.*

She watched them for a moment. They were scampering all over the yard, poking into everything with their curious little noses.

By this time, Miss Simpson decided that she was ready for her supper, too. When she was through eating, she called the kittens to come and get the meat scraps.

"I'll give you plenty to eat while you're here," she told them, "but tomorrow, back to Mr. Tooks you go."

The kittens didn't understand what she said, but they did understand what to do about the meat scraps. They purred happily.

Miss Simpson went into the front room and sat down to read the evening paper. The kittens followed her and began sniffing about the room. Soon Marmalade found the tassel on the window shade. She batted it with her paw. The tassel swung back and forth. Marmalade batted it again.

Pinafore jumped up on the windowsill, too. She caught the tassel in her teeth and began chewing on it.

"None of that!" cried Miss Simpson. "No, *no!*" And she put up the window shade so that the tassel was out of reach.

Pinafore watched that swaying tassel. Back and forth it swung. Back and forth went Pinafore's head. After a while, the tassel stopped swinging.

Pinafore jumped up on the footstool—then to the chair—then to the table—and then onto the window ledge right under the tassel.

She took the tassel in her teeth and got ready to jump down again.

Su-wish! went the window shade as Pinafore leaped. *Su-wish!*

Miss Simpson looked up. The black and white kitten seemed to be flying straight through the air, with the window shade billowing out behind her. Just then the shade caught on its roller and started to snap back.

"Let go! *Let go!*" shrieked Miss Simpson, picturing a kitten pressed flat and rolled up inside a window shade.

But Pinafore had already felt the warning jerk. She let go of the tassel and dropped to the floor. There she stood, shaking her head as if she wanted to make sure that all of her teeth were still in her mouth.

"Oh, you silly kitty," laughed Miss Simpson as she fixed the window shade.

But the black and white kitten did not watch. She turned her back to the window, as if she had never seen the tassel—and never wanted to.

Miss Simpson picked up both kittens and took them out to their bed beside the stove. "I don't know how you feel," she said, "but I've had quite a day."

Then she went to bed herself. She was just dropping off to sleep, when something landed with a *plop!* on her right foot and something else landed *plop!* on her left foot. Then she heard a soft *purr-r-r-r-r.*

"Oh," said Miss Simpson aloud. "The cats!"

The kittens came bouncing up to the head of the bed. They licked her hand as if to say, "Here you are! We looked all over for you!" Then they

90

trotted back to the foot of the bed and curled up, with their heads on Miss Simpson's toes. They made very cozy foot warmers.

"I guess," Miss Simpson murmured as she dropped off to sleep, "I guess I can try to keep them one more day."

The next day was Tuesday. After breakfast, the cats followed Miss Simpson into the sewing room. She gave them some old empty spools to play with, so that they would keep out of mischief.

When Mr. Tooks came by, she told him that she would keep the cats just one more day.

"I've named them Marmalade and Pinafore," she told him. "I hope you don't mind."

"What?" said Mr. Tooks. "Why didn't you name them Peach Preserves and Overalls?"

Miss Simpson looked hurt. Then she saw the twinkle in Mr. Tooks's eyes and knew that he was joking.

"Well," he said, "have to be going. Hope the

kitties behave themselves."

"Oh, they're playing with some spools," Miss Simpson said. "They're as good as can be."

But by afternoon the kittens were tired of the spools. They sat by Miss Simpson's feet and cried.

Miss Simpson went right on sewing.

Whirr-r-r went the motor. All of a sudden, Marmalade jumped up onto Miss Simpson's lap and then onto the machine. The next minute, Pinafore was beside her. They cocked their heads to one side and watched the needle busily moving up and down. Suddenly Pinafore put out a paw to stop the flying needle.

"Oh, *oh!*" cried Miss Simpson. "You'll be hurt."

She stopped the machine just in time. "No, no. Mustn't touch," she scolded, and she spanked Pinafore's paw and put her down on the floor. "Be a good kitty, like Marmalade," she started to say, but she didn't, for Marmalade wasn't being a good kitty. She had the thread in her mouth

93

and was unwinding the whole spool.

Miss Simpson spanked more than Marmalade's paw. Then she put both cats out in the kitchen.

"You're going back to Mr. Tooks the first thing tomorrow morning," she said as she shut the door.

"Meow!" came from the other side of the closed door. "Meow! Meow!"

Miss Simpson went back to work, but after a while, she began to realize that the cats had been very quiet for a very long time.

"I wonder what they're up to," she said. She tiptoed to the kitchen door and listened. Not a sound. She opened the door a crack and saw Pinafore asleep beside the stove. She opened the door wider. There sat Marmalade in the sink. The orange kitten was holding out her paw to catch the water from the dripping faucet, and she was busily washing her face!

Miss Simpson giggled. At the sound of her

voice, both cats came running to meet her. They rubbed against her legs and purred loudly.

"Why, look at that," said Miss Simpson. "I believe you're glad to see me."

The kittens purred louder, and all afternoon they were as good as kittens can be. They took catnaps in the sunshine. They played with the spools. They chased their tails.

After supper, Miss Simpson sat down to read the evening paper. The kittens came and curled up in her lap, as if they belonged there. After a while, Miss Simpson went to start the water for her bath. The kittens followed her. As usual, they had to look into every corner of the room.

They put their paws on the edge of the bathtub and stared at the splashing water. They jumped up on the rim of the tub and walked around it. Miss Simpson went into the bedroom.

All of a sudden she heard a *SPLASH! Splish-splash!*

They've fallen in! thought Miss Simpson, and

95

she rushed for the bathroom.

Just as she reached the door, a wet orange streak whizzed past her. A black and white streak was right behind it.

The streaks whizzed across the room and hid under the bed. Miss Simpson got down on her knees. Two sets of gleaming eyes stared back at her. The kittens were soaking wet—but not hurt. They were so big-eyed with surprise that Miss Simpson burst out laughing.

"Curiosity killed a cat," she said. "I've often wondered what that old saying meant. Now I know."

In a little while the kittens came out. Miss Simpson rubbed them dry with a soft towel. The kittens began to purr. Marmalade reached up and patted her chin. Miss Simpson put an old blanket across the foot of her bed and laid the kittens down on it gently.

Somehow on Wednesday morning, Miss Simpson just didn't happen to see Mr. Tooks go by.

So, of course, she couldn't give the cats back to him.

On Thursday morning, Mr. Tooks came along as she was watering the petunias by the gate.

"Good morning," he called. "How are Apricot Jam and Apron?"

She was so busy scolding him for saying the wrong names that she forgot to tell him that she thought two cats were too many.

On Friday morning, Miss Simpson put the cats out in the yard while she did her weekly cleaning. When she was through, she sat down on the porch to rest.

There was a rustling in the bushes beside the path. Out jumped Marmalade.

"Nice kitty," began Miss Simpson. Then her eyes and mouth opened wide. Marmalade was carefully carrying a gray mouse up the path!

"Ee-e-ee!" screamed Miss Simpson and leaped up onto the porch railing.

Marmalade was so surprised that she dropped

97

the mouse and ran up the nearest tree. Pinafore ran after her.

"Ee-e-ee!" screamed Miss Simpson. She was still screaming when Mr. Tooks came by.

Mr. Tooks carried off the dead mouse. He helped Miss Simpson down from the railing. He brought her a drink of water.

"There, there, now," he said, patting her hand.

When at last she was calm, they both started looking for the cats. There they were, way up on a high branch of the big elm tree.

"Hey, come down," called Mr. Tooks.

"Here, kitty, kitty," called Miss Simpson.

Pinafore tried to back down. But her hind legs wouldn't quite reach to the next branch. Marmalade tried to slide down headfirst. But her legs were too short, too. "Meow!" they said. "Meow! *Meow!*" But they did not come down.

Mr. Tooks pushed his hat to the back of his head and pulled his left ear. "Hmm," he said. "Looks bad. But 'tain't hopeless. I guess I still know how to climb a tree."

He took the letters and packages out of the mailbag and slung the empty bag over his back. Up the tree he went.

In a few minutes, Mr. Tooks and the mailbag with Marmalade and Pinafore in it were safely back on the ground. The kittens scampered off, as lively as ever, but Mr. Tooks was all out of breath.

"I can't do that very often," he said with a shake of his head. "Tell you what you need—a nice boy."

"A what?" said Miss Simpson.

"A boy," said Mr. Tooks. "And I know just where you can get one. My sister is in charge of the Children's Home up at Coal City, you know. I'm going up there tomorrow. Which do you want me to bring you—a boy with blue eyes, or one with brown?"

"Oh," said Miss Simpson, "I don't—"

"My sister says," Mr. Tooks was going on,

"that city kids just love going to a small town like this. She'll be right pleased to hear that you want to take a boy."

"But I—" began Miss Simpson again.

"Oh, just for a week or two," Mr. Tooks added quickly. "The boy can look after the cats until they're big enough to climb down trees by themselves. The boy will help you, and you can give the boy a real vacation. It's terrible for those poor city kids to be cooped up all summer."

"Yes," said Miss Simpson kindly. "It is a pity."

"There," said Mr. Tooks, beaming. "I knew you'd do it. I'll bring back a nice boy Sunday night."

Then he was off down the street before Miss Simpson could say that she didn't want a boy at all. She wasn't even sure that she was going to keep the cats.

On Saturday morning, Miss Simpson was up bright and early. Since she couldn't stop Mr. Tooks from bringing a boy, she decided to make the best of it. But what would she and a strange boy talk about? "I'll just keep him busy eating," she decided. "Whenever I don't know what to say, I'll offer him something to eat."

She got out eggs and flour and sugar and her best currant jelly and started to make a jelly roll. The cats climbed up on a stool. They watched every move she made.

"Meow!" they said, as if to remind her that it was high time they got something to eat.

"Nothing for you," she told them. "I have a boy to feed." She put them out into the yard, but she kept looking out so often, to make sure they didn't climb the big elm tree, that she almost let the cake burn!

Maybe a boy will help, she thought. *I wonder what color eyes he'll have. I never did tell Mr. Tooks which color I like.*

She made some custard to go with the jelly roll. Then she went upstairs to fix up her brother's old room.

101

She was so busy that Sunday night came almost before she was ready, and there was Mr. Tooks, ringing the doorbell. Three long rings and a quick one.

She smoothed back her hair and hurried to open the door.

"Oh," said Miss Simpson. "Oh, my!"

There beside Mr. Tooks were *two* boys!

"You didn't say which you wanted," said Mr. Tooks. "Blue eyes or brown. So I just brought both. Tim and Bud."

The boys grinned.

Miss Simpson swallowed hard. "W-W-Welcome home," she stammered. "W-Would you like some jelly roll?"

Tim and Bud slept late the next morning, but Pinafore and Marmalade saw to it that Miss Simpson was up on time. She put the cats out in the yard and got quite a bit of sewing done before she heard the boys coming downstairs.

Miss Simpson scurried to the kitchen and began to get their breakfast. There were big bowls of fresh peaches and cream, and there were pancakes, maple syrup, bacon, and tall glasses of milk.

"Gee," said Tim, the blue-eyed boy. "It's swell of you to ask us. I've never been in a home like this."

"Neither have I," said Bud, the brown-eyed boy. "You're tops."

They kept eating until Miss Simpson began to think that pancakes would pop out of their ears.

"Whew!" said Tim at last. "I'm full."

"So am I," said Bud. "Where are the kittens? You know, I've always wanted a kitten."

The kittens acted as if they had always wanted boys. They crawled all over them. They licked their hands. They tugged at their shoelaces. Miss Simpson told the boys how the kittens had climbed the tree and couldn't get down.

"We'll fix that," said Bud. "I saw something in

103

a movie once that gives me an idea."

"That's fine," said Miss Simpson. She tried to think of something else to say. She couldn't offer them food—not after that breakfast!

But Tim had an idea of his own. "Let's go play in the yard," he said.

Bud tucked a kitten under each arm and followed Tim outdoors.

Miss Simpson sighed—and began to bake a chocolate cake. Mr. Tooks was coming for lunch, so she wanted to have something special.

At ten o'clock she looked out to see what the boys and the cats were doing. The cats were walking along the top of the high board fence. Right behind them were Tim and Bud, their arms held out like tightrope walkers at a circus.

Miss Simpson shut her eyes and waited for the crash. Nothing happened. She opened her eyes. The boys—and the cats—were safe on firm ground.

Those boys! she thought. *They can worry me*

*more than cats, any day. Mr. Tooks will have to
take them back the first thing tomorrow morning!*

She finished icing the cake and went upstairs
to make the beds. Suddenly she saw her market
basket fly past the bedroom window.

Miss Simpson blinked her eyes and rubbed
them.

As she opened her eyes, the market basket
flew by again. She could scarcely believe what
she saw. Was that really her basket going past
the window?

"El-e-vator," came Tim's voice from the
ground outside her window. "Elevator. Going
down."

Miss Simpson rushed to the window. Marmalade and Pinafore and Bud were up in the elm
tree. So was her market basket. Bud was putting
the kittens into the basket. Tied to the basket
was her clothesline. On the ground below, holding the other end of the clothesline, was Tim.
When Bud gave a signal, Tim slowly let the rope

out. Down to the ground went the basket and the kittens.

"See our elevator?" said Bud. "We'll train the cats to climb in by themselves. Then you can let them down out of the tree as easy as pie."

"Want to try it?" Tim offered.

Miss Simpson gulped. "Would you like some jelly roll?" she managed to say.

When she got downstairs, the boys had already helped themselves.

Marmalade and Pinafore were up on the boys' laps, begging for their share.

"M-m-m," said Bud. "Best jelly roll I ever ate."

"I'll say," Tim agreed. "Gee, you're the best cook in the world, Miss Simpson. What I mean, THE BEST."

Bud sighed. "Wish I could stay here. We could go fishing, maybe. I bet you could cook fish just right, Miss Simpson."

"Why can't we go fishing today?" asked Tim. "We can dig worms first. Huh, Miss Simpson?"

107

Worms! Miss Simpson shuddered.

Just then the doorbell rang. Three long rings and a quick one. Miss Simpson turned and ran. She opened the door and got outside on the porch before Mr. Tooks had a chance to move.

"What's the matter?" he asked.

"The boys," said Miss Simpson. "They want to stay—"

"Fine," said Mr. Tooks. "Wonderful. I told my sister you might—"

"Wait," said Miss Simpson. "It's not wonderful. It's terrible. They want to go . . . fishing."

"What's terrible about that?" asked Mr. Tooks.

"Worms!" said Miss Simpson. "Wiggly, crawly WORMS!"

Mr. Tooks pushed his hat back on his head and pulled his left ear. "Hmm," he said. "That is bad. But 'tain't hopeless. Tell you what you need —a husband!"

"What?" gasped Miss Simpson, turning as pink as the petunias. Then her eyes twinkled.

Those Cats!

"How many?" she asked. "One—or two?"

"ONE!" said Mr. Tooks. "And I'm the one. How about it?"

Miss Simpson swallowed hard. "C-Come in," she said. "Come in and have some jelly roll!"

THE CAT WHO PAID HIS WAY

Alice Means Reeve

Toby sat on the front steps of his grandfather's house. He was feeling sad and lonely. He was wishing he had someone to play with.

Grandpa and Grandma had gone to town. Toby had stayed home, in case anyone telephoned or came asking for Grandpa to do some work for them.

Toby watched cars passing. They were all colors. Some were going fast, some slow. A yellow taxi went by. Suddenly the taxi stopped. It backed up and stopped in front of the house. A man got out of it and hurried through the gate in the picket fence and up the front walk.

"Hi there, young fellow!" he called. "How would you like to have a cat?"

Toby jumped down off the steps, and his brown eyes began to shine.

"Oh, boy!" he said. "You mean to keep?"

"Yes," the man said. "Come and see him."

Toby followed him to the taxi. There on the backseat was a cat, but it was not like any cat Toby had ever seen before. It was the color of a peeled banana, and it had a chocolate brown face, feet, and tail.

"Is that a *cat?*" Toby asked.

"Yes, it's a Siamese cat—only a year old. I just got a job in South America, and I can't take him with me. I promised to give him to some friends, but they've just found out they can't keep pets in their new apartment. My plane leaves in an hour. I saw you sitting on the steps looking lonely, and I thought he might be as good a pal to you as he's always been to me."

111

"Can I hold him?" Toby asked. He was so excited that his voice squeaked. Imagine having a cat of his very own!

The cat wore a little blue leather collar with a silver bell on it. A blue leather leash was fastened to the collar. The man put him in Toby's arms.

The cat snuggled close to Toby and began to purr loudly. Then he reached up and gently licked Toby's chin with his rough pink tongue.

"See, he likes you," the man said. "His name's Shah."

"Shah," Toby said. "Shah." The cat looked up and licked him again.

"I'd like to speak to your mother," the man said. "I want to ask her if it's all right for you to keep him."

"I live with my grandpa and grandma, and they've gone to town," Toby said. "But *please* let me keep him. I *know* they won't mind, and I'll take awfully good care of him."

The man thought for a minute. He looked at

his watch. "If I don't hurry, I'll miss my plane," he said. "Well, if you're sure they won't mind, then he's your cat now."

Toby nodded his head, too excited to speak. He tightened his arms around Shah.

"Oh, I forgot one thing," the man said. "He likes to leap on people's shoulders. It might frighten you if you didn't know about it. Long ago, in Siam, cats like Shah guarded the royal palace. They used to patrol the tops of the walls, and sometimes they leaped on their enemies."

"Gosh!" Toby said, and his eyes almost popped out of his head.

The man took Shah from Toby. He put him on the ground. Then he pointed to Toby's shoulder. Shah leaped onto it. He stood there, rubbing his furry face against Toby's cheek. He made a cheerful little trilling sound.

"Take good care of him," the man said. "He likes to eat canned salmon and liver and cream and sometimes a little chicken. I guess I've

113

got to admit I spoiled him a little."

He reached out and rubbed Shah behind the ears. He said sadly, "So long, fellow. I'm going to miss you." Then he got into the taxi, and the driver went zooming down the street on his way to the airport.

Toby put Shah down on the ground and began to walk up and down the sidewalk with him. Shah trotted along on his leash like a small dog. He stopped to nibble a blade or two of tender green grass at the edge of the walk. Then he lay down flat on the sidewalk and wouldn't go any farther.

"Get up, lazy Shah," Toby said. But the cat shut his eyes as if he were tired. He just lay there.

So Toby picked him up, which was just what Shah wanted. He opened his blue eyes wide and licked Toby's face. He purred loudly, obviously pleased with his new owner.

It was the happiest sound Toby had ever heard. It made him feel good to hear it. He could

114

even *feel* the purr throbbing under his hand.

Pretty soon Toby heard Grandpa's old pickup truck come rattling down the street. Grandpa drove it into the shed in the backyard.

Grandpa McGee was a fine carpenter, but sometimes he was so cross and grumpy that people didn't like to hire him. He was a tall, strong man with a gray moustache. When he was cross, it turned down at the ends. When he was happy and laughing, it turned up and changed his whole face. It hadn't turned up for a good long time now.

Toby ran into the backyard, carrying Shah.

Grandpa and Grandma climbed out of the pickup truck. Toby jumped up and down in excitement. "Look what I have," he said. "His name's Shah, and he's mine!"

Grandpa saw Shah's small brown face peeping out from Toby's arms. He shouted, "We're not going to keep any monkeys around *here!*"

Toby laughed. He put Shah down on the

ground so they could see him. "It isn't a monkey," he said. "It's a *cat*—a Siamese cat!"

"Where did you get him, Toby?" Grandma asked.

"A man in a taxi stopped and gave him to me," Toby said. Then he told them everything the man had said to him.

Grandpa was looking grumpy and mad—and a little sad, too. "We can't keep him, Toby," he said. "I don't have much work these days, and we can't keep anybody who doesn't pay his way. We all have our chores to do. You bring in kindling and set the table and wipe the dishes for Grandma. But what can a fancy cat like that do to earn his bed and board?"

Toby picked up Shah and hugged him. He said, "But, Grandpa, he's so little. He wouldn't eat much. Just canned salmon and liver and cream and sometimes a little chicken, the man said."

"Hoity-toity!" Grandpa shouted. "Who does

117

this society cat think he is? Canned salmon and liver and cream and chicken, indeed! That's a lot better food than *we* get to eat!"

Grandma was looking more and more worried. She put her hand on Grandpa's arm. "Hush, Patrick," she said. "Do you want everybody in town to hear you yelling? No wonder nobody wants you to work for them anymore, when you act like this! You're bellowing like a foghorn!"

She put her arm around Toby's shoulders and patted Shah's soft fur. "Grandpa's just worried," she said. "We'll have to keep the cat tonight, anyway. Then, in the morning, we'll see if we can find a good home for it."

Grandpa mumbled something and carried the groceries into the kitchen. Then he sat down tiredly in the old rocking chair by the stove. "Come here a minute, Toby," he said.

Toby was still holding Shah in his arms. He went over and stood by the rocker, hoping that Grandpa might be changing his mind.

118

"We just can't keep him, boy," Grandpa said. "But don't look so sad. I promise you this: Someday, when times are better, I'll get you a regular cat or maybe a dog."

"But I want Shah," Toby said. "He loves me, and I love him."

Grandpa sighed. "Most everybody wants things they can't have, Toby," he said. "You'll just have to make the best of it."

Grandma gave Shah some warm milk and a little of the stew that had been cooking all afternoon. Shah took a few laps of the milk. He washed his face, his paws, and the backs of his ears. Then he curled up in a tight little ball behind the stove and went to sleep.

Toby felt so unhappy that he could hardly eat. When dinner was over, he wiped the dishes for Grandma. Then he went down the stairs that led from the kitchen into the basement. He stood near Grandpa and watched him as he busied himself in his workshop.

Grandpa could build anything, and he was proud of his fine tools. He kept them oiled and sharpened and free of rust. Some were in racks on the walls. Some were in drawers in the long workbench.

He was making a kitchen window box for Grandma, so she could grow parsley and other herbs in it. He rubbed it smooth with sandpaper as he said, "A man's no better than his tools, boy. Have to keep 'em in good shape if you want to do good work."

"Can I help you?" Toby asked.

Grandpa said, "Of course you can. The younger you learn, the better carpenter you'll be when you grow up."

So he gave Toby a piece of fine sandpaper. He let him rub the window box. He told him to rub it until it was as smooth as glass.

"If there's ever a fire here," Grandpa said, "my tools are the first things to save." He turned back to his work.

Toby was kneeling on the floor, working. Suddenly Shah leaped up onto his shoulder. He rubbed against Toby's cheek.

Toby reached up and hugged the little cat. Then he said, "Grandpa, *please,* can I keep him?"

Grandpa looked sad. He looked cross, too. His moustache turned way down. "No," he said. *"No!"*

The loud noise frightened Shah. He leaped off Toby's shoulder. He went skittering sideways across the cellar floor, with stiff legs and arched back. His eyes glowed like two red taillights on a car, and his ears were laid back flat to his head.

Even though he was feeling unhappy, Toby couldn't help laughing.

Then Shah began to act like a furry grasshopper. He leaped onto the workbench and then onto Grandpa's shoulder. Grandpa jumped and grabbed for the cat, but he was gone again, sailing through the air like a bat. He leaped up onto a beam. He whisked through the air and landed on top of the furnace. His eyes gleamed, and his chocolate brown tail puffed up like a bottle brush. Then he began to say things in his loud, hoarse voice.

Toby giggled. "I think he's calling you names, Grandpa," he said.

"Silly cat's crazy as a June bug!" Grandpa muttered. He looked over his shoulder uneasily.

Just then Grandma called to Toby that it was time to go to bed.

"Can I take Shah to bed with me, Grandpa?" Toby asked.

"No!" Grandpa said. "I'd just as soon have a live tiger in the house! He can stay down here tonight. I'll shut the kitchen door, so he won't come up and scare us all to death with his leaping around and wailing like a banshee!"

Up on top of the furnace, Shah stopped scolding. Then he sat there for a minute, watching the tip of his tail move. Suddenly he began to chase it, going round and round in circles.

Toby laughed again, and Grandpa said, "Go to bed, boy."

Toby whispered, "Good night, Shah," and went upstairs.

He said good night to Grandma and went to bed. He was thinking that he would give almost anything in the world if he could keep Shah. Shah, with his rough pink tongue and his loving ways and his silly tricks that kept you laughing— a pet like that could make a big difference in a boy's life.

Toby kept thinking how lonely Shah would be, down there in the cellar all by himself, but he soon fell asleep, tired from the excitement.

Sometime in the middle of the night, Toby was awakened by a horrible noise. It was a cross between a scream and a roar of pain. It was so loud and so frightening that he sat straight up in bed like a jack-in-the-box. He began to shake all over. He jumped out of bed. Then he ran out into the hall and bumped into Grandpa.

123

"Get back in bed, Toby, till I see what all this racket is about!" Grandpa yelled.

Grandpa ran into the kitchen and flung open the cellar door. He went down the stairs. Toby could hear his big bare feet going *plop-plop-plop* and shaking the house.

Suddenly Toby thought of Shah all alone down there in the cellar. He was afraid something might have hurt him. So, instead of going back to bed as his grandfather had told him to do, Toby followed him. His small bare feet made hardly any sound at all.

Grandpa clicked on the cellar light. Following along behind him, in his candy-striped pajamas, Toby saw a strange sight—a sight that he would remember all his life.

There in the cellar, right in front of Grandpa's workbench, was a big fat man in his stockinged feet. He was yelling and struggling. He was trying to shake something off one shoulder. The *something* was Shah. He was clinging as tightly

to the man's shoulder as a burr to a dog's tail, and he was scolding angrily in his loud, hoarse voice.

The man saw Grandpa McGee, who looked about eight feet tall in his long nightshirt. He started to dive through the window, but Grandpa reached out his long, strong arm and grabbed him. Just then Grandpa saw a big brown sack on the floor. Sticking out of it were some of his tools.

Grandpa was so mad that he shook the burglar till his teeth rattled.

"Steal *my* tools, will you?" Grandpa yelled and shook the man some more, outrage making him stronger than ever.

Shah had clung to the burglar's shoulder till Grandpa grabbed hold of the man's arm. Then he jumped onto the workbench. He sat down and began washing his paws and face with quick, short licks. His tail was big and round, and it was lashing angrily. In the dim cellar light, his

126

eyes shone like two rubies.

Grandpa, still shaking the burglar, yelled, "Toby, go phone the police. Hurry!"

Toby ran up the stairs so fast he almost flew. But when he got to the hall, Grandma was already phoning. Then she hung up and said they were sending a police officer right away.

Toby went flying down into the cellar again. Grandpa was making the burglar take all his tools out of the sack. He made him put them back where he found them.

Toby called Shah very softly. Shah stopped washing behind his ears. He leaped down from the workbench, light as a feather, and ran to Toby, murmuring little greetings of recognition as he came.

Toby picked him up and held him tight. Shah snuggled against him and began to purr like a miniature motor. Then he reached up and licked Toby's chin.

They went upstairs, and Grandma fixed some

warm milk for both of them. Then she made Toby go to bed.

"You can take Shah to bed with you," she said. "But tomorrow we have to find a new home for him."

Toby and Shah were snug in bed, when they heard the siren of a police car coming closer. The car stopped in front of the house. Toby heard Grandma hurry down the hall and open the front door. Then there was the sound of tramping feet and loud voices.

Toby held Shah close. He told him what a brave cat he was. And then, even though Toby was a pretty big boy, a few tears fell on Shah's soft coat. Toby couldn't forget that Grandpa was going to send the little cat to a new home in the morning.

The next thing Toby knew, there was sunlight coming in the window. Just outside, in the old apple tree, a blue jay was chattering.

128

Toby thought he'd had a bad dream. Then something moved beside him. There was Shah, washing a paw in the sunshine. He leaned over and licked Toby's face lightly with his little sandpaper tongue. He began purring.

Toby gave him a big hug. Then he got up and washed and dressed. He went out into the kitchen to breakfast. Shah trotted after him, sniffing the air as if he were hungry, too.

"Well, well, good morning, Toby," Grandpa said.

They all sat down and began to eat their oatmeal. Suddenly there was a loud knocking at the back door. Chief Masters, of the town's police, came in.

"*Good* morning, everyone," he said. "I have a little piece of news for you. That burglar you caught last night was the Cat Burglar. Creeps in and out of people's houses in his stockinged feet, he does. He's a bad one. Been looking for him for months."

129

"Trying to steal my tools!" Grandpa grumbled. "How can a man work without his tools? Not that the likes of *him* would care!"

Chief Masters was smiling at Grandpa. "I have a surprise for you, Patrick," he said. "Would you like to ride down to the police station with me and find out what it is?"

"Well, well," Grandpa said, getting up from the table. "A surprise for *me?*" He looked pleased and rubbed his hands together.

The chief said, "It's a fine morning. How would you *all* like to ride downtown in the police car?"

"Oh, boy!" Toby cried, jumping up and down. "I've never ridden in a police car before! Can Shah go, too?"

"Of course he can!"

Toby got Shah's leash. He snapped it on the blue collar with the bell. Grandma got her hat. Then they all got into the shiny police car. It was warm, so they opened all the windows.

130

Chief Masters drove slowly. The siren made a soft *eeeeeeeeeeeee-eeeee* sound. People on the sidewalk turned around to see what was going on. Grandpa laughed and waved, and the people waved back. Toby thought this must be how it felt to be in the lead car of a parade, so he waved, too. He even waved Shah's paw at the people.

A man called out, "Hey, Mr. McGee, my wife's been wanting a new back porch built on our house. Can you do it for us?"

"Of course I can!" Grandpa shouted. "Be there bright and early tomorrow morning."

The chief stopped the car in front of the police station, and they went inside. He got something out of his desk drawer.

"Well," he said, showing his teeth in a big smile, "here's the surprise. There's a hundred-dollar reward offered for the capture of the Cat Burglar. I have the pleasure of presenting it to *you*, Patrick McGee. And here is the money. Ten brand-new, crisp ten-dollar bills."

131

For the first time in months, the ends of Grandpa's gray moustache really turned up with happiness. He stood there holding the crisp new bills. They made a pleasant crackling sound as he fingered them.

"Grandpa!" Toby said, and he tugged at his grandfather's sleeve. "Grandpa, that isn't your money!"

"Nonsense, boy! Of course it's my money! I caught the Cat Burglar, didn't I?"

"No, you *didn't!*" Toby said. He almost jumped at the loud, angry sound of his own voice. "Shah caught him. That's Shah's money!"

For a minute Grandpa's face looked like a thundercloud. Toby thought maybe Grandpa would give him a good hard spanking. But then Grandpa's gray moustache twitched. Suddenly he slapped his leg and broke into a great roar of laughter.

"Ha!" he shouted. "Cat catches Cat Burglar. That's good!"

Chief Masters began to laugh, too. Then Grandma started to laugh. But Toby didn't laugh.

Pretty soon Grandpa wiped his eyes with the back of his hand and sat down on a bench. "I haven't had such a good laugh for months," he said. "Makes me feel like a new man. But how could a *cat* use money?" He stuffed the bills in his pocket.

Chief Masters said he would drive them all home again. They climbed into the police car, all except Grandpa. He said he had an errand to do and he'd be back in a minute.

Pretty soon he came back with some packages. He got into the car and said, "Let's go!"

The chief started the car. They went riding down the street, with the siren going softly again. A woman on the sidewalk saw Grandpa looking so jolly and called to him.

"Mr. McGee," she said, "I've been wanting a new set of shelves in my sewing room. Can you make them for me?"

134

"Indeed I can, Mrs. Jones, ma'am," Grandpa said. "I'll be there bright and early next Friday morning."

When they got home, they thanked Chief Masters and went up the front walk. Shah trotted along on his blue leash, just like a small dog. But halfway to the porch, he lay down suddenly. He shut his eyes and wouldn't get up again.

Grandma said, "Oh, the poor little thing! In all the excitement, he didn't get any breakfast this morning, and I haven't a thing in the house for him to eat."

Grandpa laughed. Then he waved the packages he was carrying. He said, "But *I've* got something. I've got canned salmon and liver and cream and chicken!"

Toby's eyes almost popped out of his head. "But, *Grandpa,* you said—"

"Never mind what I said," Grandpa interrupted. "Poor cat's weak from hunger."

So Toby picked up Shah, which was just what

135

Shah wanted. Then they all went in and watched him eat his canned salmon and liver and cream and chicken. But Toby still felt like crying. After all, today Grandpa was going to find a new home for the little cat.

When Shah finished eating, he sat up and washed his face and his paws. He washed behind his ears, then licked the tip of his chocolate brown tail. Then he jumped up into Grandpa's old rocking chair. He curled up into a tight little ball and went sound asleep.

Grandpa said, "Well, have to go downstairs and sharpen my tools. Lots of new jobs coming up." On the way, he walked past Toby and rumpled his hair.

"What are you looking so sad about, boy?" he asked.

Toby felt tears in his eyes. "You said we'd have to find a new home for Shah today. But, Grandpa, *can't* I keep him, instead? Please? Oh, please?"

136

"*Keep* him!" Grandpa roared. "Well, I'd just like to see anyone take him away from you! Good smart watchcat—pays his way just like anybody else! Of *course* we're going to keep him!" He leaned down and patted the warm fur ball with one rough hand.

Toby felt a smile spreading over his face—a smile so big that it made his ears wiggle.

"By the way," Grandpa said, "I've got some money here that doesn't belong to me." He took the ten crisp, crackling ten-dollar bills out of his pocket. "After lunch I'll drive you and Shah downtown. You can go to the bank and start a bank account under both your names. How's that? I bet there won't be another cat in town with a bank account!"

Then Grandpa went clumping down the cellar steps, chuckling to himself. "Cat catches Cat Burglar," he said. "That's a good one!"

Toby stroked the sleeping cat. He was the happiest boy in the world. He had a wonderful,

137

brave, loving cat of his very own—and both he and his cat were rich!

Shah opened one blue eye for just a second. Toby giggled, because it looked exactly as if Shah were winking at him.

YOU WILL ENJOY

THE TRIXIE BELDEN SERIES

22 Exciting Titles

THE MEG MYSTERIES

6 Baffling Adventures

ALSO AVAILABLE

Algonquin
Alice in Wonderland
A Batch of the Best
More of the Best
Still More of the Best
Black Beauty
The Call of the Wild
Dr. Jekyll and Mr. Hyde
Frankenstein
Golden Prize
Gypsy from Nowhere
Gypsy and Nimblefoot
Lassie—Lost in the Snow
Lassie—The Mystery of Bristlecone Pine
Lassie—The Secret of the Smelters' Cave
Lassie—Trouble at Panter's Lake
Match Point
Seven Great Detective Stories
Sherlock Holmes
Shudders
Tales of Time and Space
Tee-Bo and the Persnickety Prowler
Tee-Bo in the Great Hort Hunt
That's Our Cleo
The War of the Worlds
The Wonderful Wizard of Oz